SLS

Supporting Lea...

D0534101

Hampshire
County Council

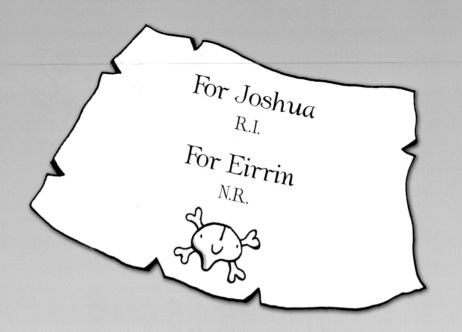

For Joshua
R.I.

For Eirrin
N.R.

Reading Consultant: Prue Goodwin, Lecturer in Literacy and
Children's Books at the University of Reading

ORCHARD BOOKS
338 Euston Road, London NW1 3BH
Orchard Books Australia
Hachette Children's Books
Level 17/207 Kent Street, Sydney NSW 2000

First published by Orchard Books in 2008
First paperback publication 2009

Text © Rose Impey 2008
Illustrations © Nathan Reed 2008

The rights of Rose Impey to be identified as the author and
Nathan Reed to be identified as the illustrator of this Work
have been asserted by them in accordance with the
Copyright, Designs and Patents Act, 1988.

A CIP catalogue record for this book is available from the British Library

ISBN 978 1 84362 975 7 (hardback)
ISBN 978 1 84362 983 2 (paperback)

1 3 5 7 9 10 8 6 4 2
Printed in China

Orchard Books is a division of Hachette Children's Books,
an Hachette Livre UK company.
www.hachettelivre.co.uk

Pirate Patch
and the
Gallant Rescue

ROSE IMPEY • NATHAN REED

ORCHARD BOOKS

Patch was in a bad mood.
He couldn't wait until he was
a *proper* pirate.

"Pirates shouldn't have to go to school," he grumbled. But suddenly Patch stopped grumbling – something was wrong.

Pierre *wasn't* on his perch. Portside *wasn't* waiting at the gate. And Granny Peg *wasn't* digging holes in the garden as usual.

Inside the house Patch
found two of his crew
tied up – and gagged!

Creeping Crayfish!

On the table was a ransom note.

Bring us the
Treasure Map...
or your GRANNY is FISH FOOD!

Signed: Your sworn enemies

"It's from Bones and Jones,"
Patch growled.
"That *scurvy* pair!"

Patch untied his crew and
picked up the treasure map.
Then he and his crew set sail
in *The Little Pearl* to
rescue Granny Peg.

In a few flaps of Pierre's wings, they found Peg, tied up on a sandbank.

Peg, ahoy!

They were only just in time. The tide was creeping closer by the minute.

Patch was a brave little pirate. He didn't stop for a minute before mounting a *Gallant Rescue*.

It was a pity Patch didn't
stop, because the minute he
left his ship . . .

. . . the *villainous* Bones and Jones crept aboard.

The cunning pair quickly sailed
away in Patch's ship, taking Peg's
map with them. They left Patch
and Peg stranded.

As *The Little Pearl* disappeared,
Patch shouted all the things he
would do when he caught up
with those pesky pirates.

Back on board *The Little Pearl*,
Bones and Jones were already
fighting about who should have
the map.

I'm the biggest!

I'm the oldest!

While, below deck, Portside,
the cleverest sea dog ever to sail
the seven seas, was hiding.

He was busy making a clever plan.

Suddenly Bones and Jones heard *strange* noises coming from below: "Whooo! Whooo!"

They stopped fighting over the map. They started fighting instead over who should go below to investigate.

In the end, the scurvy pair went together. They opened the cabin door and peered nervously inside. But it was too dark to *see* anything.

Whoooooooooo!

G-g-great gannets!

The noises were getting louder.
"This ship's h-h-haunted!" they
both h-h-howled.

The next moment a ghostly white
shape shot between the pirates'
legs. It was wailing
and whining.

Bones and Jones were so scared
they jumped overboard. They
swam for the shore – followed
by a shoal of sharks.

Then Portside, that clever sea dog,
sailed back to the sandbank.
He was just in time to rescue
Patch and Granny Peg!

THE LITTLE PEARL

"Wait till I get hold of those cheating good-for-nothings!" yelled Patch.

But that adventure would have
to wait for another day. Mum
and Dad's ship was just coming
round the headland.

Patch had to get home before they knew he'd been gone.

"How was school?" asked Dad.
"I hope you've been good,"
said Mum.

Patch smiled and nodded and
looked more like a little angel
than a little pirate.
If Mum and Dad only knew . . . .

★ Pirate Patch ★

ROSE IMPEY   NATHAN REED

All priced at £4.99